This book belongs to

THE CAVE TWINS

By Lucy Fitch Perkins

ILLUSTRATED BY THE AUTHOR

WALKER AND COMPANY
New York

448818   5140

CONTENTS

THE CAVE TWINS

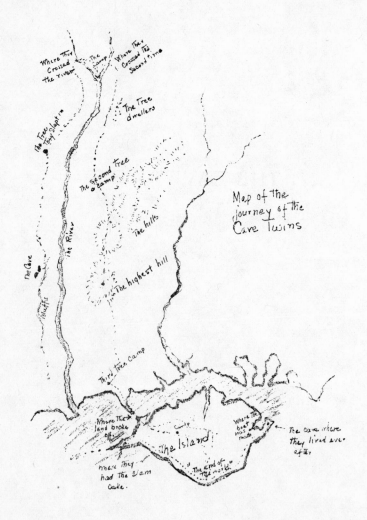

Where They
Crossed
the River

The
Camp

Where They
Crossed the
Second time

The Tree
Slept in

The Tree
dwellers

The Second Tree
o'camp

Map of the
Journey of the
Cave Twins

The River

The Cave

The hills

The highest hill

Bluffs

Third Tree Camp

Where the
land broke
off.

Camp

The Island!

Where the
boat was
made

The Cave where
they lived ever
after

Where they
had the clam
Cake.

"The end of
the world"

PREHISTORIC MAN

This is a story about things that happened ages and ages ago, before any of us were born, or our great-great-grandfathers either, for that matter. It was so very long ago that there were no houses, or farms, or roads from one place to another, and there was not a single city, or a town, or even a village in the whole earth.

There was just the great, round world, all fresh and new, and covered with growing things; and there were wild beasts of all kinds in the forests, and fishes of all kinds in the seas, and all sorts of birds and flying creatures in the air.

Besides all these wonderful things in the new, new world, there was Man.

He was quite new too. He did n't know much of anything about the world. All that he really knew was that there was a world, and that he was in it, and that there were fierce wild animals in it too, which would kill him and eat him if he did n't kill them first. And he knew very well that he was not as swift as the deer, or as big as the elephant, or as

I

strong as the lion, or as fierce as the tiger, and it seemed to him as if he had n't much chance to stay alive at all in a world so full of terrible creatures who wanted to eat him up.

But this Prehistoric Man was very brave, and he could do two things which none of the other creatures could do — he could laugh and he could think.

One day, he sat down on a rock, and took his head between his hands and thought and thought, and by and by he lifted up his head and said to his wife, — for of course he had a wife, — "I have it, my dear. If we are not as strong as the wild beasts, we must be a great deal more clever."

So he got right up off the rock and set about being clever. And so did his wife. They were so clever that they hid themselves in trees and rocks where the wild beasts could not find them. And they found out the secret of fire.

The other creatures could not find out the secret of fire to save their lives, and they were dreadfully afraid of it. Then the Man and his wife made weapons out of stones, and bones, and they made dishes out of mud, and though these things were n't a bit like our weapons or our dishes, they got along very well with them for many years.

2

In the earliest times of all, the Woman hunted and trapped the wild creatures, and fished, all by herself, but by and by she began to let the Man do the hunting and bring home the game, while she stayed in the cave house and kept the hearth-fire bright and took care of the children. She cooked the food that he brought home, and she made needles out of bones and sewed skins together for clothes for her husband and the children and herself. After a long time she began to plant seeds of the wild things that she found were good to eat, and to raise food out of the ground.

All these things they did, and many more that had never been done before, — and because they were so much more clever than all the beasts of the forest, the Prehistoric Man and his prehistoric wife lived a long time in a little peace and more happiness than you might at first think possible.

They taught their children all the clever things they had thought out, and these children, when they grew up, taught them to their children, and this went on for hundreds and thousands of years. Each generation learned new things and taught them to the next, until now we have houses and churches and villages and cities dotted over the whole earth, and there are roads going from everywhere to everywhere

else. There are railroads and steam-cars and tele-
graph and telephone lines, and printing-presses, so
that to-day everybody knows more about the very
ends of the earth than Prehistoric Man could possibly know about what was happening fifty miles
away from him.

And all these things we have to-day because the
Prehistoric Man and the Prehistoric Woman did
their part bravely and well when the earth was
young.

This is a story about that far-off time. If you
don't believe it's true, every word of it, just get out
your atlas and find the places on the map. They are
every one of them there.

I
GRANNIE AND THE TWINS

I

GRANNIE AND THE TWINS

ONE bright morning of early spring, long ages ago, the sun peered through the trees on the edge of a vast forest, and sent a shaft of yellow sunlight right into the mouth of a great, dark cave. In front of the cave a bright fire was burning, and on a rock beside it sat an old woman. In her lap was a piece of birch-bark, and on the bark was a heap of acorns. She was roasting them in the ashes and eating them. At her right hand, within easy reach, there was a pile of broken sticks and tree branches, and every now and then the old woman put on fresh wood and stirred the coals to keep the fire bright.

A little path ran from the front of the cave where the old woman sat down the sloping hillside to a blue river, and the morning sun shining across it made a bridge of dazzling light from shore to shore.

Beyond the river there were green fields and forests, and beyond the forests high hills over which the sun climbed every morning. What lay beyond those far blue hills neither the old woman nor any of the clan of the Black Bear had the slightest idea.

Everything seemed quiet and peaceful on that spring morning so long ago. The trees were beginning to turn green and little plants were already pushing their way through the carpet of dead leaves. A robin lit upon the branches of a tree above the cave and sang his morning song.

There was no other sound except the sizzling of a wet stick on the fire, and the snapping noise made by the old woman when she took a roasted acorn from the fire and cracked it with her teeth.

The old woman was not pretty to look at. Her face was as brown as leather and covered with wrinkles, and her hair hung about it in ragged gray locks. It was no

6

wonder that her hair was rough and ragged, for it had never been combed her whole life long, and she was quite old — oh, as old as forty, maybe! But she really couldn't help her hair being like that any more than she could help being forty, because there was not a single comb yet made in the whole world!

It was a mystery how she cracked the nuts so well, because she had only a few teeth left in her mouth. For clothing she had nothing but the skin of a deer fastened over her left shoulder by a thorn, and tied around her waist with a leather thong.

Although she seemed to be thinking of nothing but her nuts, the little bright eyes of the old woman kept close watch in every direction, and her ears were quick to hear every unusual sound. If a twig snapped, or there was a rustling noise in the under-brush, she was ready in an instant to fling fresh dry sticks on the fire and make it glow red against the black opening of the cave.

She knew that no wild animal, however fierce and hungry, would dare come near the leaping flames. Yet watchful as she was, she did not see two children who were creeping stealthily toward her, over the great rocks which sheltered the mouth of the cave.

They were a boy and a girl, and from their size they must have been about eight years old. They both had bright twinkling eyes and flaming red hair, and were dressed alike in skins of red foxes of almost the same color. You could tell at a glance that they were twins, but it would have puzzled any one to tell whether they were both boys or both girls, or one of each kind. They came down over the rocks so quietly that not even the quick ears of the old woman heard the faintest sound.

When they had almost reached the ground, they stopped, and at the same instant opened their mouths and howled exactly like two young wolves!

The noise was so sudden and so near

that the old woman never thought of her
fire at all. She simply screamed and fell
right over backwards into the cave. Then
she rolled over and scuttled on all fours
out of sight in the darkness as fast as she
could go.

The acorns from her lap flew in every
direction and rolled down the hillside. The

boy and girl jumped to the ground, shrieking with laughter. In a moment the old
woman was back again in the door of the
cave. She had a stout stick in her hand
and she looked very angry. She shook the
stick at the Twins and scolded them so fast
that the sound of it was like the chattering
of an angry squirrel in a tree-top.

Now, of course, I cannot tell you just the

words she used, but, translated into English, this is what she said: —

"You horrid little catamounts, if I catch you, I'll teach you better manners! I'll give you such a taste of this stick that you'll not need more till the river runs dry."

The Twins sprang up, still shrieking with laughter, and danced about the fire just out of reach of the woman's stick.

"But you can't catch us," they screamed.

Their red locks of hair flew about in the wind as they danced, until it looked almost as if red flames were bursting from their heads. The old woman glared at them helplessly.

"Dance away," she cried, "dance away, you red-headed rascals! I shan't need to put sticks on the fire while you are here. Your red hair would scare away the saber-toothed tiger himself! No wonder you are not afraid to run alone in the forest! With such heads on you, you are as safe as if you were in the heart of the cave."

Just then she saw her acorns all spilled on the ground, and her rage broke out afresh.

"Pick them up, you little rats! They are the last of my winter's store, and it will be four moons yet before they will be ripe again."

Down went the children on their hands and knees, and began to gather up the scattered nuts. Young as they were, they knew the value of food. They also knew the taste of Grannie's stick. In those days food could be found only at the risk of life itself and was not to be thrown away while hunger lasted.

Besides, the hunting had not been good for some time. The reindeer had gone farther north, and the great herds of bison had not yet come back from the warmer regions, where they ranged in winter. There were wild beasts of many other kinds in the forest, but the hunters of the clan had not brought home meat for several days. This was one reason why the children had ventured so far into the forest. Most of the time they and the other children of the clan stayed near the cave under the watchful eye of the old woman, while their fathers and mothers went hunting.

"Now, don't be cross, old Grannie-sit-by-the-fire!" cried the girl. At least, I think it was the girl, but the Twins looked so exactly alike I can't be quite sure. "We'll pick up your nuts for you. And if you'll

put your stick down, we'll give you something we brought for you."

The old woman's face softened. You
might almost have thought there was the
beginning of a smile in the corners of her
mouth, but she only said, "I know your
tricks, worthless ones! You have brought
me nothing but a fright and a tumble in the
ashes."

The girl poured the acorns she had gathered into the piece of birch-bark which
served the old woman as a plate, and
danced over to the mouth of the cave. She
saucily took the stick out of Grannie's hand
and flung it on the fire, and then led her
back to the stone seat.

"Go along and get it, Firetop," she called.
I know it was the girl who said this, because
it was the boy who was called Firetop, on
account of his red hair. The girl's hair was
just as red, but they called her Firefly.

Firetop sprang up the rocks down which
he had climbed so carefully only a few mo-
ments before, and came down again slowly,

carrying something in each hand. He stood
before the old woman with his hands behind him.

"Guess, Grannie, guess!" cried Firefly.

By this time, the smile had got out of the corners of Grannie's mouth and had spread all over her face.

"Roots," she said.

"Wrong," shouted the children. "Guess again."

"Spruce gum."

"Wrong again," laughed the Twins.

Grannie thought a while this time. Then she said, "Snails."

"No, no, no," the Twins said both together; and then Firetop slowly brought his hands round in front of him and showed the old woman four large bird's eggs.

You should have seen Grannie's face then! It was all wreathed in smiles, and when she smiled she was n't so bad to look at after all. Almost nobody is for that matter.

She took the eggs from Firetop's hands and covered them carefully in the ashes.

"We'll roast them," she said. "I've had nothing to eat but acorns for three days

16

past. Now, tell me where you have been, and how you found the eggs."

"We were hungry," explained Firetop, "and all the big people had gone off hunting, and we thought we'd go too. We thought we knew where we could find some roots. So we hid ourselves and waited until Robin and Blackbird and Squaretoes had gone down to the river to hunt frogs, and then we ran back into the woods." Robin and Blackbird and Squaretoes were the other children of the clan.

Firefly could never stay quiet for very long and now she broke into the story.

"Yes, and we found some roots, too," she said. "We were just eating them when from a hazel bush right in front of us we heard a loud snort! We didn't wait to dig any more roots, I tell you! There was a chestnut tree nearby, and we grabbed a limb and swung ourselves up just in time. It wasn't only one, it was *three* wild boars that rushed out of the bushes, and the biggest boar had tusks as long as this."

Firefly held up a stick about eight inches long, as she spoke.

"It's lucky we were up in the tree, for they were all hungry too, and they looked as if they thought Firetop and I would taste very good," she laughed. "Then Firetop teased them. He hung down from the limb and tickled their noses with a long stick. My, but they were mad!"

"Yes," said Firetop, "they looked just as mad as you did, when we scared you, Grannie."

"I wonder one look at you didn't scare them to death," said Grannie, "because animals are so afraid of fire! I am used to the flames on your heads, but if I were to come upon you for the first time I think I'd climb a tree myself! Or else I should think the woods were on fire and run away."

Grannie poked Firefly in the ribs and laughed at her own joke.

"Maybe our red hair helped some," said Firefly, "for pretty soon they all three turned and ran grunting off through the woods."

"And then," said Firetop, "we thought
we'd come back by the tree path. We went
out on the limb of the chestnut as far as we
could go, and swung into the big oak tree
that stood next. There are a lot of oak trees
together there and we were going along

from one to the other, when there was a loud whirring noise and a big bird flew out of the top branches right over our heads! We looked up and saw the nest. It was made of sticks. I got the eggs and handed them down to Firefly, and then we came home."

"You didn't come all the way by the tree path and carry the eggs, did you?" cried Grannie admiringly.

"Oh, no," said Firefly. "The eggs were too big to carry in our mouths. So Firetop dropped to the ground and I handed the eggs down to him. Then we ran back home as fast as we could."

"You will be as great hunters as your father and mother one of these days if you keep on," said Grannie. "And no one in the whole clan can do better than they can. My, my, I can remember when your father was a boy, how he used to hunt eggs! That's how he got the name of Hawk-Eye. He could find eggs, and other things too, where nobody else could find anything at all. How he could swing along through the trees! No wild creatures could ever get the start of him. And then your mother! She could run faster than the wind could blow. She wasn't easily scared, I can tell you. She had always her legs to depend upon! I've seen her run from a mad buck so fast that she made just a streak of light through the forest. And when the buck got too near, she swung herself into a tree and then hung by her legs safe above his head and teased the buck crazy because he could not reach her. Ah! She was a wild one in those days, and well she earned her name of Limber-leg!"

"I'm sure the eggs must be done by this time," said Firetop.

Grannie reached down and poked the ashes away from the eggs. They were very hot, but her hands were so tough and horny that she could even handle live coals. She gave one egg to Firefly. Firefly took it in her hand, but her hands were not quite so tough as Grannie's and it burned her like

everything! She dropped it on the ground,
squealing with pain. It was cooked so hard
that it did not spill, though the shell was
broken. Grannie laughed.

"Aha," she said, "I'm even with you
now for giving me such a scare."

"Ho," boasted Firetop, "that's nothing.
Watch me! I guess if you can handle them
I can." He reached down and picked up
an egg and held it in his hand. It was just

as hot as a coal of fire, but he pretended it didn't hurt him. He cracked and ate it in two bites, and though I'm sure it must have burned a red path all the way to his stomach, he never said a word. But when Firefly wasn't looking he did suck the air into his mouth to cool his tongue!

"Grannie can have the other egg, can't she, Firetop, because we scared her so," said Firefly, when they had each eaten one.

"You may scare me every day that you bring me bird's eggs," said Grannie.

Grannie took the last egg from the ashes and was just cracking it when suddenly there was a shout which made them all jump. Those were pretty jumpy times, I can tell you, for a new sound might mean almost any kind of danger. There were so many wild beasts in the forest that no one could feel safe a single minute unless he was deep in a cave. Even then the cave had to have an entrance so narrow that no man-hunting animal could get into it, or

23

else a fire must be kept burning before it to frighten them away.

The moment they heard the sound, Grannie dropped her egg and sprang to her feet. Firetop and Firefly popped into the cave and were out of sight in an instant. Grannie threw fresh sticks on the fire, and as it blazed up, she looked fearfully about in every direction. Now she heard another sound besides the shouts and screams of children's voices. From far away down the river came a long low roar and the tramp, tramp of many feet. A group of children came tearing up the path toward the cave, shouting at the top of their lungs, " The bison are coming, the bison are coming!"

Grannie took up the cry. " The bison are coming, the bison are coming!" she shouted into the cave, and out tumbled Firetop and Firefly in the twinkling of an eye.

"Where, where?" they screamed.

" There, there, in the river bottom," panted Squaretoes, the biggest of the boys. "We were hunting for frogs and all of a

sudden there was a roar, — at first so faint
we could hardly hear it, — then far down
the river we saw them coming! Run, run
to the big rock, and you can see them
too."

Grannie threw a great heap of dry wood
upon the fire and ran with the children to
the big rock, which lay part way down the
path toward the river. From the top of this

rock the whole valley was spread out before them like a map.

Squaretoes pointed toward the south, and there in the green marshy land bordering the river were hundreds and hundreds of great dark hairy beasts. They were running, and as they ran, they made a low roaring sound that was frightful to hear.

"We shall have fresh meat to-night," said Grannie to the children. "The herd has been frightened. I could not see the leaders. Some of our hunters have surely found them."

They stood on the rock until the great herd had thundered by and was out of sight around a bend in the bluff. Then Grannie said, "Come, let us go back to the fire and gather plenty of fuel, so we can cook the meat when it comes, and have a great feast."

II

THE BISON FEAST

II

THE BISON FEAST

FOR hours Grannie and the children worked together to get a huge pile of fuel ready for a feast which they hoped to have at night. It was something like getting ready for Thanksgiving.

"It is likely that old Saber-tooth will be having a feast too," said Grannie. "He is as glad as any of us to see the bison come back. Maybe now he won't catch any bad children who stray too far into the wood."

You see, the fierce saber-toothed tiger was the beast they feared most of all, but they always had to be on the watch for wolves and hyenas, and for the dreadful cave bear as well. There were wild horses, too, and elephants, and mammoths, and lions. Grannie had to keep telling the children about these dangers, just as our mothers tell us to-day to keep out of the way of trolley-cars and steam-engines and automobiles. Only trolley-cars and steam-engines don't run after us and stick their heads right into our front doors and try to eat us up, as the wild creatures did in those days.

It seems to us now that no one could possibly have had any happiness in a world so full of dangers, but you see Grannie and all the rest of the clan did not know that life could be any different. Just because there were so many dangers, they grew brave to meet them, and a brave man among dangers is far happier than a coward in a safe place. So perhaps they had just as good a time living as we do, after all.

By the time the children had gathered a heap of wood large enough to cook the biggest kind of a feast, it was afternoon. There was nothing in the cave to eat, and they grew hungrier and hungrier, but there were no signs of any hunters. Shadows began to gather in the woods. Now and then there

was a cry of some night bird, or of a distant wolf. These were lonely sounds. Firefly began to be discouraged.

"Suppose they should n't bring home
any meat after all," she said.

"Then we'll just have to go hungry,"
said Grannie.

Firetop laid his hand on his stomach and
groaned.

"*Men* never complain of such things,"
said Grannie.

Firetop took his hand off his stomach at once and made believe he had just coughed a little. You see the cave people taught their children to bear hunger and pain without making any fuss about it.

"I tell you what we could do," said Grannie. "If we had some water, we could have a place to boil the meat all ready when the hunters come back. Who'll go for water?"

"I'll go," said Firetop.

"So will I," said Blackbird.

"And I," said Squaretoes.

They were all boys. Robin and Firefly were the only little girls in the clan.

"Get the gourds and the pig-skin and run along, then," said Grannie. "Keep a sharp lookout, for you know the wild beasts will soon be out for their night hunting."

Firetop ran for the skin of the wild boar which was in the cave. It was their water-cask. The other boys got gourds with holes cut in them to make dippers, and then they were ready to start.

Grannie took three sticks of pine and laid the ends in the fire. When they were burning well, she gave one of them to each of the boys for a torch.

" It is n't dark yet, but you will be safer with these, anyway," she said.

As soon as the three boys had gone skipping and whooping down the path to the river, Grannie and the girls set about getting a kettle ready. They hollowed out a hole in the ground, not far from the fire. When it was deep enough they lined it with a heavy piece of hide. They put stones around the edge of it to keep it in place. Then they gathered piles of small stones and threw them in the fire to get hot. By the time all this was done the boys were back with the pig-skin full of water. Grannie poured it into the hollow dish in the ground.

It was almost dark, and it seemed to the children that they could not wait another minute, when they heard a welcome sound. It was the noise of voices, talking and laughing together.

They sprang to their feet and gave a whoop of joy. It was answered by a shout from the path.

"They are coming slowly and they are laughing. They have meat," cried Grannie. She threw more wood on the fire. Up flew the flames, lighting the forest with a red glare. Sparks floated away over the very tree-tops. By its light they saw Hawk-Eye and Limberleg and all the other men and women of the clan toiling up the path. The bigger boys were with them, too, and they were all loaded down with great chunks of bison meat!

The weary hunters dropped the bison-skins in one place to be stretched and cured the next day. The meat they threw down on the ground at the mouth of the cave, and Grannie and the other women began at once to cook it.

Some of it they put in the fire to roast and some of it they put in the leather kettle in the ground. Then they poked the hot stones out of the fire into the water. They kept taking the stones out of the water with sticks as they grew cool and putting them back into the fire to get hot again. In this way they soon got the water to boil.

The smell of the roasting and boiling meat was too much for Firetop. It made him so hungry that he couldn't wait. He just snatched a piece of meat from the ground and ate it raw! But he was ready to eat again when the meat was cooked and the real feast began.

Then the great fire blazed and crackled outside the entrance and filled the cave with a warm red glow. The whole clan gathered in the front of the cave near the fire.

Hawk-Eye was the leader of the clan, because he was the strongest man and the best hunter. He was a large man with little sharp eyes and red hair which covered his breast and legs as well as his head. Around his neck was a string of bear's teeth.

There were four other men. They were called Eagle-Nose, Gray Wolf, Big Ear, and Long Arm. There were three other women besides Limberleg and Grannie. They were the wives of the men. There were four big boys, who were already hunting with the men, and there were Blackbird, Robin, and Squaretoes, besides Firetop and Firefly. These were all there were in the clan of the Bear.

When the feast began, the people all sat down in a circle, all but Grannie. Grannie stood up and handed out great chunks of meat to the others and kept the fire bright. But she had a bone in her hand all the time, and whenever she had a chance, she gnawed it. There were no knives or forks or plates, of course. They all took their meat in their hands and just gnawed and gobbled as fast as they could! Nobody had any manners, and not a single mother said, "Have you washed your hands?" or "Don't take such large mouthfuls or you will choke yourself," or anything like that. There were some things about those days that must have been very pleasant, after all.

For a long time they ate and said nothing. You see, food had been scarce for so many days that they had to make up for lost time. But by and by, when they were all stuffed full, Firetop rolled over on to the skin of a bear which was lying on the cave floor, and said to his father: "Tell us about the hunting. Who killed the meat, and how was it you all came back together? Did you hunt in a pack, like the wolves?"

"Not just like the wolves," said Hawk-Eye, laughing. "There were five of us after the bison. The women went off to set snares for rabbits, and the boys to hunt eggs along the bluffs up the river. I felt in my bones that we should see the bison to-day. So the men and I took our way toward the lowlands. We knew they would come from that direction. We followed the bluffs for a long way, but found nothing. We were beginning to think we should come home empty-handed, when far away I heard bellowing. Then I saw a little black speck moving along the green

36

valley. Two black specks moved beside it. They were the leader and his two sentinels, and behind them came the herd."

"We saw the herd, too," cried Firetop. "I saw them first," said Squaretoes. "I saw them just as quick as you," shouted Blackbird.

"Shut up," said his mother, and Blackbird did. Fathers and mothers in those days used just such language as that, and if the children did n't mind at once, they were likely to get something worse than just language. It was n't a polite age at all.

"We crept down the bluffs as quietly as snakes," went on Hawk-Eye, when everybody was still again. "I was in front. When the leader of the herd got to our hiding-place, I sprang from the bushes and threw my spear with all my strength. He gave a mighty roar. He stood on his hind legs and thundered. Then Big Ear sprang forward and threw his spear. The leader fell. The herd broke and ran. The sentinels could not control them. Then we ran toward them. We killed two young cows with our axes. The rest of the herd rushed past. The leader and the two cows were left behind. The leader was old and tough. We pulled out our spears and left him to the jackals and hyenas. The two cows were small. We skinned them and cut them into pieces and started for the cave. At the foot of the path we met the other people. They were weary and had caught nothing. When they saw us they laughed for joy."

"We heard them," cried Firefly. "Grannie said you would bring meat. She said so when we heard the laughing. She said so when the herd passed by. She saw that they had been frightened. That is why we had the kettle ready."

"Grannie is a wise old woman," said Hawk-Eye. "Now, get to bed, every one of you."

The children scuttled away and threw themselves down on heaps of skins which lay about the cave, and were soon sound asleep. At least the others were asleep, but for some reason Firetop and Firefly stayed awake. Maybe they had eaten too much. At any rate they lay in their corner, on their own heap of skins and watched Hawk-Eye and Limberleg and Grannie and the others as they sat about in the cheerful glow of the fire. Nobody had said anything for a long time, and the Twins were beginning to feel quite sleepy, when Hawk-Eye spoke. What he said made them sit up and listen with all their ears. Of course neither Hawk-Eye nor Limberleg thought for a moment that the Twins were awake or listening. Grown people are often very stupid about such things! Anyway, they were awake, and they did listen, and this is what they heard.

Hawk-Eye said, "I am going across the river to-morrow."

"Why are you going?" asked Big Ear.

"I want to see what lies beyond the blue hills that the sun climbs over," Hawk-Eye answered.

"But no one of our clan has ever gone across the river. Our hunting-grounds have always been on this side," said Long Arm.

"It's time some one did go, then," said Hawk-Eye. "Game will be plentiful now everywhere, but after the reindeer go, there is a long time that we have little food. We need to find new hunting-grounds. I am going to seek them."

"Then I am going, too." It was Limber-leg who spoke. "I can hunt. I can trap as well as anybody. And I can throw a spear as straight. I am not afraid. Grannie will look after the children while we are gone."

When he heard that, Firetop poked Firefly in the ribs.

"I am going with them," he whispered.

"They'll never let you," Firefly whispered back.

"I'm going anyway," Firetop answered. "Don't you tell."

"If you go, I'm going," said Firefly. "I can go as well as you can."

"Sh-sh-sh—" said Firetop, for Grannie was speaking.

"The river is wide and dangerous," she said. "The current is swift, and who knows what monsters may be in it? I myself saw a rhinoceros wallowing in the mud only a few days ago. Some say they have seen a serpent as large as the trunk of a tree."

"We can go up the river until we find a shallower place to cross," said Hawk-Eye. "I have killed a tiger and a rhinoceros and a cave bear in my time. We can take care of ourselves."

When Limberleg heard him say "We" she knew that she was going, and she was glad. She was as brave as Hawk-Eye and almost as good a hunter.

When they saw that Hawk-Eye had really made up his mind to go, nobody else said anything. They knew it would be a waste of words; and in those days there were fewer words to waste than we have now.

"We must start early," Hawk-Eye said to Limberleg. "We will take one extra skin apiece and our axes and spears."

Limberleg rose at once and went over to the corner of the cave where the Twins were. The Twins shut their eyes tight and pretended to be sound asleep. Firetop even snored a little. Limberleg spread the skins of two bears upon the cave floor and threw herself on one of them. Hawk-Eye went to the cave-mouth, took a look at the stars, yawned, warmed himself at the fire, and then he too went to bed. The rest of the men and women found their own places in other shadowy corners of the cave, and soon the whole clan of the Bear was sound asleep.

III
THE RUNAWAYS

III

THE RUNAWAYS

NEXT morning Firetop awoke before the dawn. He sat up at once and looked about him. Not another soul was stirring, and from the different corners of the cave came the sound of snores. The fire was burning brightly, for Grannie had been up four times in the night to put on fresh fuel. Now she too was fast asleep. Firetop crawled quietly out of the warm wolf-skins of his bed. He took one of the wolf-skins and tied it over his shoulder with a leather thong. The rest he bunched up to look as if he were still in bed and asleep.

Hawk-Eye had made a small spear for each of the Twins. They were not play-things. They were real spears, for children of that day had to learn to use such weapons while they were still very young.

45

Firetop took his spear in his hand and poked Firefly gently in the ribs with it. She woke instantly and would have poked back if Firetop had n't shaken his head at her and laid his finger on his lips. She nodded, crawled out of her bed, and bunched it up like Firetop's. Then she tied a wolf-skin over her shoulder and took her own spear, and together the two children crept silently past the sleepers and out of the cave. They snatched chunks of meat from the remains of the feast as they passed.

It was not yet daylight, though the sky was pink above the hills across the river and all the birds were singing as the Twins came out of the cave and ran down the river path. Neither one of them spoke until they were far enough from the cave so that no one could hear them. Then Firetop whispered: "We'll climb a tree. We can watch from the tree and see when they start. Then we'll slide down and follow them. They won't know we are with them until it's too far to send us back."

"They won't like it," said Firefly. "What
do you think they will do to us?"

"They'll wallop us," said Firetop, "but I
don't care. It won't hurt when it is over, and
I've just got to go. We shall see all kinds
of things that we've never seen before."

"Well," sighed Firefly, "I do hate that
part of it, but I guess it's worth it. Come
on. Let's climb this tree."

The children could climb like monkeys,
but they had their weapons and the meat

and that made it a little difficult. They leaned their spears against the trunk of the tree, took the meat in their teeth, and up they went as easily as you could go upstairs. Then they hid themselves in a fork of the tree and ate their breakfast.

The thick branches made a screen around them so they could see without being seen. They watched the cave. It was not long before they saw Grannie come out and take a look at the weather. Then she put more fuel on the fire and sat down on a rock to gnaw a bone for her breakfast.

Soon Hawk-Eye and Limberleg appeared. They each had their weapons, and a reindeer-skin strapped by leather thongs across their shoulders. Limberleg had a gourd tied to her belt. They were each gnawing bones, too. They stopped to speak to Grannie. The Twins leaned forward and listened with all their ears. They heard Hawk-Eye say, "The children are still asleep. You can tell them when they wake up."

Then they came along the path, eating as they came. They passed almost under the tree where the Twins were hiding. This seemed to the Twins so funny that they stuffed their mouths full of meat and then clapped their hands over them to keep from laughing aloud. As it was, a little snicker ran out between Firefly's fingers. Hawk-Eye heard it.

"What's that?" he said sharply. He and Limberleg stopped a moment and listened.

"Nothing but a squirrel," said Limberleg. "There he is on that log over there."

The Twins nearly smothered themselves then, to keep the laughs in.

Hawk-Eye and Limberleg passed on down the path to the very edge of the forest. There they turned and walked along the bluffs, where they could swing themselves into a tree at a moment's notice. This was safer than walking in the green meadows beside the river where there were no trees to climb.

Firetop and Firefly waited until they were out of sight around the turn. Then they crawled down from the tree, took their spears in their hands, and ran after them. They stayed back far enough so they could hide behind trees if Hawk-Eye or Lim-

berleg should turn round, yet near enough
to keep them in sight.

For miles and miles they walked and ran.
It was hard with their short legs to keep
the pace set by their father and mother, but
they knew very well they had to do it. There
was no turning back then.

On and on walked Hawk-Eye and Limberleg. The sun climbed higher and higher. The children were thirsty, but they did not dare to run down to the river for a drink. They were hungry, but they had nothing to eat. They snatched little green leaves from the bushes as they passed, but this was hardly enough to fill their empty stomachs.

"We'll just have to call them," said Firefly at last. "I'm so hungry I've simply got to have something to eat, and if we stop to hunt for roots, we'll never catch up with them again."

"They'll be as mad as mad bulls when they see us," said Firetop.

"Yes, of course. We'll get a good beating," answered Firefly. "We expected that. But it won't hurt after it is over; you told me so yourself."

"Jimminy!" said Firetop, — or if it wasn't "Jimminy" it was something that meant the same thing — "I just hate to think of it. Can't you go on a little longer?"

"What's the difference?" moaned Firefly. "It's got to come some time. We might

as well have it over. I'm not going another
step." And she sat plump down on a fallen
tree.

Firetop put his hands to his mouth and gave a long sharp cry. It was the distress signal of the Bear Clan. Hawk-Eye and Limberleg stopped instantly. They looked up the river; they looked down the river. Then they caught a glimpse of two red heads and two very scared faces, far back on the bluff. They came tearing back through the underbrush to the two small figures on the log.

They could hardly believe their eyes.

"Where did you come from, you naughty little weasels?" cried Limberleg angrily.

"From the cave," said Firefly. "We followed you because we want to see what lies beyond the blue hills across the river, too. And if you are going to spank us, please do it right away, because we are awfully hungry."

"Oh, no," cried Firetop. "You need n't do it now if you 'd rather not! Could n't you put it off until we get home again? We 're willing to wait, and you 'd have more time then."

Limberleg and Hawk-Eye did n't discuss the matter. They sat right down on the log and began. Limberleg took Firefly and Hawk-Eye took Firetop, and they spanked and spanked.

"Now, can we have something to eat?" sniffled Firetop when it was over. Limberleg looked at Hawk-Eye. "We can't send them back alone," she said. Firetop saw that they were going to give in.

"The hyenas would surely get us," he said plaintively. "We're pretty small to go back alone," sobbed Firefly. "And besides, we want to see what lies beyond the blue hills across the river."

It may be that Hawk-Eye was a little pleased at their courage in following them. Anyway, he said: "Well, you can climb like squirrels. We shall not be gone many days. Come along." Firetop sprang up and whooped for joy. Firefly turned a somersault. Hawk-Eye and Limberleg laughed. They could n't help it. You see, even in those early times parents were fond of their children, although they did n't know any better punishment for them than spankings. There are some parents like that yet.

"Now, what shall we have to eat?" said Firefly, when everybody was happy again.

"We 'll have to find something," said Hawk-Eye to Limberleg. "You take the children down into the meadow. I see carrots growing down there. I 'll hunt in the woods. Listen for my call, and when you hear it, come to that big oak tree as fast as you can."

Limberleg and the Twins started at once down the bluff toward the river. The bushes grew thick along the slope, and as they scrambled through them they made a crashing noise. Firetop was ahead, then came Firefly, and last of all Limberleg.

Suddenly there was a loud whirring sound, and out of the bushes in front of them flew a great wood grouse!

Instantly Firetop braced himself and flung his spear, and before Limberleg or Firefly could catch up with him, he was far

56

beyond them down the slope, struggling
with the wounded bird. When they reached
him, he had killed it. Limberleg was delighted. She patted Firetop and called him
a great hunter, and said she was glad he
had come with them after all.

Maybe you think Firetop was n't a proud

boy then! He waggled his red head and swaggered up the slope toward the big oak tree with the huge bird on his shoulder. Limberleg and Firefly stayed behind to hunt in the bushes for the grouse's nest. Firefly found it, and there were seven eggs in it! Then Limberleg patted Firefly. "Your father and I will not need to get any food for you," she said. "Maybe you will hunt for us." They went up the slope after Firetop, carrying the eggs.

When they reached the big oak tree on the bluff, Limberleg took the feathers off the grouse and cut it into chunks with her flint knife. They had no fire, so they ate it raw. They ate five of the eggs and left two for Hawk-Eye. They saved the legs of the grouse for him, too. They waited and waited, but still Hawk-Eye did not come. They began to get a little frightened, he was gone so long. At last there was a call, "Hoo, hoo, hoooooo," like the hooting of an owl, and he appeared crashing through the bushes. He had a rabbit hanging from

58

his shoulder. Then Firefly played a trick
on him.

"We aren't hungry," she said. Hawk-
Eye was astonished.

"I thought you were starved by the way
you acted," he said.

59

"We aren't any of us hungry now," said Firetop.

"Did you fill yourselves with carrots?" asked Hawk-Eye.

"Oh, no. We had fresh meat," said Firetop, with his nose in the air.

"Fresh meat?" cried Hawk-Eye.

"What did you kill?" he said to Limberleg.

"Nothing," said Limberleg.

"But I did," shouted Firetop.

He told all about killing the grouse. You should have seen Hawk-Eye then! He was just as pleased as our fathers are when we get A in arithmetic!

"I guess you can take care of yourselves," he said, when he had heard the story. "You don't need me." Then he laughed and made his face look scared. "Will you let me go with you to the land where the sun rises?" he said. "I am very small, but I can climb trees! I am afraid to go alone. I need you to kill bison and mammoths for me to eat!"

Firetop, Firefly, and Limberleg laughed at this until they nearly choked. Then Firetop wagged his head at his father.

"You should n't have followed me," he said. "I shall have to spank you. But you are too small to send alone to the cave, so I 'll have to let you come with me."

IV
THE JOURNEY

IV

THE JOURNEY

I

ALL the rest of the day they followed the river, looking for a place where it was shallow enough for them to cross without serious danger of drowning. They did not know how to swim. For their supper they had only the rabbit. They ate it sitting on the bluff, with their backs to each other so they could watch in every direction for signs of danger. When the shadow of the bluff grew long across the meadows, Limberleg said: —

"Darkness will soon be upon us. Where are we going to sleep?"

"We won't sleep in a cave anyway," said Hawk-Eye, "even if we could find one. We might find the cave bear at home in it. In that case, we should probably spend the night in his stomach, and I am sure that would be too crowded to be comfortable."

"We can't spend the night on the ground surely," said Limberleg. "Or we might wake up in the stomach of old Saber-tooth instead." This was just their way of joking, because I never heard of any one waking up after being swallowed, except Jonah and Little Red Riding Hood's grandmother. And of course, this story happened long before either Jonah or Red Riding Hood or her grandmother did.

Hawk-Eye took out his flint knife. I almost said he took it out of his pocket, because it seems queer to think of a man without pockets. Of course, he didn't really have any, though. The flint knife was fastened to his belt by a thong.

"Go and find all the grape-vines you can," he said. Limberleg and the Twins flew back into the forest to search for vines. There were plenty of them, and they pulled up a great heap of long, tough stems, and

brought them back to Hawk-Eye. Hawk-
Eye had another bunch which he had cut.
On the bluff overlooking the valley there
was a great oak tree with giant branches
spreading in every direction.

"We'll sleep here," said Hawk-Eye.
"Nothing can harm us unless a wildcat or
some such climbing creature should visit
us, and I think I could make him wish he

had n't come. I shall have my spear beside
me and shall sleep on the lower limbs."

"Shall we roost like the birds?" asked
Firefly anxiously.

Limberleg laughed, and took a leap into
the air, and caught one of the branches.
She swung herself into the tree and ran
along the branch to the great thick trunk.

"Hand up the vines," she called down,
"and I will show you how we will roost."
Hawk-Eye tossed them up to her. She

climbed higher in the tree and found a place where two limbs came together like those shown in the picture: She wove the vines back and forth over the two branches until she had made a rough net-work like a very coarse hammock.

"Now, up you come," she called to Firefly, "and I will put you to bed."

Firefly climbed the tree. This was the way she went upstairs to bed.

Limberleg took off the wolf-skin which was still tied over her shoulders, and spread it over the vine hammock. Then Firefly crawled into her bed. Her mother took the leather thong which had been around the wolf-skin and tied her securely to one of the limbs with it. That was her way of tucking her in so that she would not fall out of bed. She did n't hear her say her prayers, because in those days they did n't know there was anything to pray to, unless it was to giants, or the spirits of water or of fire, or of thunder and lightning. They prayed to them sometimes when they were frightened. I don't believe she kissed her good night, either. There was not much kissing in those days.

When Firefly was safely stowed away, Limberleg climbed farther up the tree to find a place for Firetop. But he had already found one for himself and was beginning to make his bed. When he was swung from his branches like a big cocoon, Hawk-Eye and Limberleg made themselves as comfortable as they could on the lower limbs of the tree. The western sky was all aflame with yellow and red, as they settled themselves for the night, and the birds sang them to sleep.

II

When Firetop opened his eyes the next morning, he could n't think where he was. He tried to flop over, as he could so easily do when sleeping on his wolf-skins in the cave. But he found himself securely tied. He lifted his head and looked out. The sun was just rising over the blue hills across the river. He looked down through the tree-branches to see his father and mother.

They were not there! For a moment he

thought perhaps he had dreamed it all. "I often go to all sorts of strange places when I am asleep," he said to himself. "Pretty soon I 'll wake up in the cave." He waited to wake up, but he did n't wake up. He kept right on being out of doors and up a tree, and his parents kept on being gone. Then he remembered all about everything. He called to Firefly, "Are you there?" She answered in a sleepy voice, "Yes." "Are you sure?" Firetop called back; "because Father and Mother are n't."

"Are n't what?" said Firefly, getting wider awake.

"Are n't there," Firetop answered.

Firefly lifted her head and tried to roll over. If she had not been tied she would have rolled out of bed. She looked down, too. The branches were certainly empty.

What would you do if you were to wake up in the morning and find yourself tied in bed and your father and mother gone and no breakfast ready? Well, they did just the same thing! They simply yelled. They had good strong lungs and they made a great deal of noise. When they stopped, they heard a distant shout that sounded like their own. "Ow, ow, ow." It came back to them from two different directions.

"That's not Father's voice," said Firetop.

"Nor Mother's," said Firefly.

"It's somebody's. It must be theirs. Let's call again," said Firetop.

They nearly split their throats that time. "Ow, ow, ow," they screamed, and "Ow, ow, ow," came back from the forest and the river.

"It must be the spirits of the water and the trees, mocking us," said Firetop. "It sounded just like us."

You see, they did not know what an echo was.

"I'm scared," said Firefly.

"I am too, a little," Firetop admitted.

"Let's not call any more. If we keep still, maybe the spirits won't find us," whispered Firefly.

They snuggled down in the wolf-skins and kept very still. By and by they heard a crashing sound in the underbrush not far away. They were stiff with fright. They did n't dare even to breathe. Then came a loud cry, "Hoo, hoo, hooooooo," and the crashing noise came nearer. It came right under their tree. Then somebody's voice called, "Are you awake, little red foxes, up in the tree?"

Two red heads instantly popped over the edge of the tree beds, and two voices cried out something that meant, "Oh, we 're so glad that you 've come back."

Limberleg climbed the tree and untied the children. It took them about two seconds to get to the ground, and they did n't fall down either. There under the tree they found Hawk-Eye. He was preparing breakfast. He and Limberleg had gone down to the river-bank very early and had found a whole colony of turtles. They had brought home four turtle-eggs apiece. If I were an arithmetic, I should ask how many eggs there were! It would have been of no use to ask the Twins. Neither they nor their father and mother could have told you. They had n't any of them learned to count that far. Nobody could in those days.

They made short work of the eggs, even if they could n't add or multiply or divide. When they had finished eating them, they strapped their skins on their shoulders once more and started up the river. All the morning they tramped steadily along, looking for a good place to ford it. The sun was already in the west, when suddenly Limberleg stopped at a turn in the bluff.

"See, see," she cried. "Two rivers." They all stopped and looked. The river forked at that point, or rather two smaller streams came together making one big one.

There was a high V-shaped point of land between the two streams.

"Now we can cross," cried Limberleg, joyfully. She led the way, running and leaping down the bluffs to the river's edge. The banks at this point were sandy and the

river full of stones. The current was swift,
but the water was clear and not very deep.
Limberleg ran out on the stones.

"Come," she called to the Twins. "Follow close after me." She leaped lightly over
the stones to the middle of the stream, where
the river was deepest. The children followed
part way; then Firetop stood still on one of
the stones and looked at the swirling water.

Firefly was on the next stone behind him. The stone in front looked a long way off to Firetop.

" I can't jump so far," he squealed.

" I can't either," wailed Firefly. " My legs are n't long enough."

"Jump," cried Limberleg, impatiently.

"We can't," shouted the Twins, beginning to cry.

You see, they were afraid of water, and it really was n't much wonder, for they had never even had a real bath in their whole lives. I 've known children to feel just the same way about water in these days. They can't bear it, even on a wash-cloth.

Hawk-Eye was on the stone behind them. " Jump," he shouted, " or I 'll give you something to cry for." And that was the very first time that any parent ever said that about giving them something to cry for, and they 've been saying it ever since, to my personal knowledge.

You see that, with Limberleg in front calling " Jump" and Hawk-Eye behind saying such alarming things, the Twins were in a tight place. There was nothing to do but jump. So Firetop took a flying leap, and Firefly followed him. Unluckily she came just a little too soon. She jumped on to Firetop. His feet flew out from under him, he lost his footing on the stone, and they both rolled into the cold water.

The crying they had done before was n't anything to what they did then, I can tell you. That is, as soon as their heads were out of the water again.

They might have been carried away by the current, if Hawk-Eye had n't instantly thrown his spear across to the farther shore and jumped in after them. He seized one of them with each hand and waded with them to land. Then he picked up his spear again from the ground where it had fallen.

If you will believe me, the Twins held tight to their own little spears all the time, even when they were under the water! It was all they had to hold to, to be sure, and besides, they loved those spears more than

we love dolls and roller skates and marbles and baseball, all put together.

Limberleg laughed at the dripping little figures.

"You look like a pair of water-rats," she cried. The Twins could not see anything funny in that. Little streams of water trickled down their backs, and they did n't like it. The rock that was on the point of land between the two rivers was not far away from the place where they landed.

" Let's go to the top," said Limberleg to the Twins. "That will warm you up."

It was quite a steep climb, and I wish you could see what they saw from that summit. They could look a long way up each of the two rivers and a long way down the big one. There were deep, silent woods along the shores. They looked back on the land between the two streams. They were all beginning to be hungry again by this time, and they hoped that they might see their supper wandering about somewhere over the rocks.

" We'll see who has the sharpest eyes," said Limberleg.

" I see something white right now, way down there in the bushes," said Firefly. " It's bouncing around."

"I see it, too," said Hawk-Eye. "It's the tail of a deer. There's a herd down there!" Hawk-Eye started down the rocks in a hurry. "I'll not be gone long," he called back to Limberleg. "Get a fire started before I come back."

Limberleg and the Twins watched Hawk-Eye until he disappeared in the underbrush. Then she and the children began to gather wood for the fire. Firetop found a piece of hard wood that was round. Limberleg pointed the end of it with her flint knife. Then they hunted for a piece of soft wood. In the soft wood Limberleg made a little hollow place that would fit the end of the stick.

"Now, Firefly, you stay with me," said she. "I want you to gather little tendrils of dry moss and watch beside me while I twirl the stick. The moment I tell you to, you must drop little pieces of dry moss into the hollow place in the wood. Firetop, you gather a great heap of sticks here on top of the rock." Limberleg knelt on the edge of the rock and began to twirl the stick between her hands. As she twirled, she mumbled a prayer to the fire god.

Firefly held the soft wood firmly in place

while Limberleg worked. She twirled and
twirled until a tiny thread of smoke began
to curl from the hollow. "Drop in the
moss," cried Limberleg. The smoke grew
thicker. Limberleg worked faster and faster.
Soon a tiny flame burst forth. Firefly fed
the flame with the dried moss until it was
big enough to burn little twigs and dead
leaves. Soon a brisk fire was burning.
Firetop had brought a great pile of wood

to the rock, and had also found some long willow branches to use in broiling meat.

"The fire is ready, but where is the food?" said Firefly. It was not long in coming. Hawk-Eye soon appeared climbing up the rock with a young doe on his shoulder. He and Limberleg skinned it and cut up the meat, and they had all the broiled venison they could possibly eat for supper.

"We shall have to spend the night here," said Hawk-Eye, when they couldn't eat any more. "We couldn't find a better place anyway. There is water around the rock except on the land side. We'll keep the fire bright, and we shall be just as safe as if we were in the cave."

Hawk-Eye spread the fire in a long line across the land side of the rock. He built a sort of wall of sticks and branches to feed it, and all night long it blazed and smouldered. They spread their skins on the rock and slept peacefully in its warm glow.

The next morning dawned bright and

clear, and the whole family got up with the birds. They had more venison for breakfast, and when that was out of the way, Hawk-Eye said: "We'd better get across the other river early. There's no telling how far we may have to go to-day, or what we may find on the way."

"I hate to leave this place," cried Firefly, "it's so beautiful, and I am sure there is lots of game here."

"I hate to leave the doe-skin behind," said Limberleg, "but of course I can't dry and stretch and cure it while we are traveling."

"We can carry enough meat to last us all day," said Hawk-Eye, "and that will save lots of time. We won't have to stop to hunt for our dinner."

He tied a great piece of meat over the shoulders of Firetop and Firefly and Limberleg, and took the biggest piece on his own back, and off they started.

III

It would take too long to tell you all
about what a time they had getting across
the river. It was deeper than the first one
they crossed, and if it had n't been for a
lucky accident, they might never have got
across at all. When they came to the
water's edge, Firetop saw some turtles sun-
ning themselves on a log a little way down
the stream. The log had floated down the

river and had caught against a dead branch that stuck out of the water. They were not so afraid of the water now they had really been in it.

Firetop thought it would be great fun to catch a turtle. He pointed them out to Firefly. "Come on," was all he said, but she knew what it meant, and at once the two children waded quietly out toward the log. Wading in was altogether different from having to tumble in, anyway. The turtles saw them coming, and just as the Twins reached the log, they slid off into the water. One of them found one of Firetop's big toes in the mud, and bit it.

Firetop screamed and tried to get away. Firefly did n't know what was the matter, but she screamed too on general principles, and they both grabbed at the log and tried to climb on to it. The log rolled over and got loose from the branch that held it and started down-stream, with both children clinging to it and yelling. They could n't get up on it because it kept turning over,

but they held on because it was the only
thing there was to hold on to, and Firetop
kept kicking with all his might to get away
from the turtle. Firefly did some kicking,
too, because she was trying to find the bottom with her feet and there was n't any
bottom there. The current was not very
swift at this point, and though they did n't
know it, the children were really swimming
with their legs, and they made the log go
toward the other shore.

While all of this was happening, where
do you suppose Hawk-Eye and Limberleg
were? They were chasing after them as
fast as they could go, but the children had

quite a start and got farther away every minute. The water was almost over Limberleg's head, and you know how hard it is to walk in deep water. Besides, they had the meat. The meat that the Twins were carrying got loose in their struggles and fell off in the water. Perhaps the turtle saw it and decided that it was better eating than Firetop's toe, or maybe he got homesick. I can't tell about that, but anyway he let go. The Twins kept on reaching for the bottom and kicking with all their might and screaming, too, and before long the log ran its nose into the farther bank and they seized the branches of a willow tree that hung over the water and pulled themselves up on the shore.

In a moment Hawk-Eye and Limberleg came tearing up the river-bank to them. They had come straight across the river, while the children had been carried some distance by the current. You can just think how glad they all were when they found that they were across and not a single one of them had been drowned.

When Firetop told about the turtle, Hawk-Eye laughed and laughed. Limber-leg laughed a little, too. Firetop felt pretty sorry for himself, but he was n't really hurt, and in half an hour he had forgotten to limp.

V
THE TREE CLAN

V

THE TREE CLAN

They walked a little way along the bank, looking for a good place to cross the flat, green meadow that lay between the river and the forest. Soon they came to a sort of path which led back into the woods. Hawk-Eye looked at it very carefully. He even got down and examined the wet ground at the water's edge. In the mud there were foot-prints.

"Isn't it a drinking-place for the wild creatures?" asked Limberleg.

Hawk-Eye grunted. "Like ourselves," he answered briefly. "There are people living in these woods. That's the print of a man's foot."

Limberleg looked just as she would have looked if he had said, "There's a pack of hyenas living in those woods." There was reason for it in those days. The different groups of people in the forests had nothing to do with one another, and when they met, they were much more likely to fight than to be friendly.

"Can't we go up the river-bank and not go into the woods at all?" asked Limber-leg. For answer Hawk-Eye pointed down the river. Far away in the green meadow they saw two mammoths feeding. Even at that distance they looked like giant rocks looming out of the grass. Their long ivory tusks gleamed in the sun.

"We can't go that way," said Limber-leg, "and it's no use to go back."

"We'll go up the path to the edge of the wood, then follow the river," said Hawk-Eye. "Maybe no one will see us. It's the best we can do. Be quiet and be quick."

He set off at a swift trot, his spear in his hand. The two children followed with their mother.

"I see shadows moving in the trees," said Firefly. Both twins wished very much

that they were at home with Grannie just
at that moment.

"They are following us, higher up on the
bluff," Limberleg answered in a low voice.

Hawk-Eye had seen all that they had
seen, and more, but he said nothing.

He trotted on. Just then a chunk of
mud and dirt came flying through the air
and struck Hawk-Eye on the head. Stones,
sticks, and all sorts of missiles followed.

"Keep on running," said Hawk-Eye.

They were terribly frightened, but they did as they were told. If they had looked up, they would have seen a terrifying sight. On the edge of the bluff there was a strange group of people. At least we must call them "people," though they looked more like monkeys than like human beings. They were grinning horribly and dancing about and chattering to each other. Their bodies were covered with dark hair. Their arms were long and strong, their legs short. They had little eyes set near together, and almost no forehead at all. Every one of them had something in his hand to throw at the travelers.

Hawk-Eye kept straight on. "Run," he cried. "We can't fight; they are too many."

On, on they ran, panting and breathless. A little way ahead there were some large rocks on the edge of the wood. There they might find a momentary shelter. They had almost reached the rocks, when suddenly a woman of the wild tribe let herself down out of a tree on the edge of the bluff and

made a bold dash down the slope. Before
they could stop her, she had seized Firefly and dragged her away. She got as far
as the first oak tree on the slope and had
actually snatched a limb, intending to swing
herself and Firefly into it, when Limberleg,
screaming with fury, reached the spot. Limberleg seized Firefly by one arm. The wild
woman had hold of the other.

They pulled in opposite directions and screamed, and if it had not been for Hawk-Eye, there's no telling what might have become of poor Firefly. She might have been pulled in two, or she might have been carried off and adopted into the wild clan. But Hawk-Eye was there in almost no time, and though the people on the bluff rained down sticks and stones upon them, Hawk-Eye drove his spear into the woman's arm. With a shriek of pain she let go of Firefly and dashed away into the forest.

"Run for your lives," cried Hawk-Eye, and they started again at top speed for the rocks. They reached them none too soon, for the people on the bluff, infuriated by the injury to the woman, came dashing down the slope after them. Once in the shelter of the rocks, Hawk-Eye turned and faced his pursuers. When they had almost reached his hiding-place he gave a fierce yell and threw his spear. It was a very well made spear with a bone barb on the end, and it struck the leader of the wild tribe in the thigh. With a shriek of pain he fell to the ground. Then he seized the spear and pulled it out of his flesh.

The wild tribe had no weapons but sticks and stones. They were tree-dwellers. They did not even know the secret of fire. They lived upon roots and berries and nuts, and such small game as they could catch with their hands or in snares. Their homes were rude shelters in the trees. When they saw what had happened to their leader, they were terribly frightened. They turned and ran for the trees, leaving the wounded man on the ground.

Hawk-Eye ran out from behind the rock, picked up his spear, and sent it flying after the enemy. It struck another man. Howling with pain and fear, he too dropped in his tracks. His companions ran faster than ever, and when they reached the trees, instantly swung themselves up by the branches and disappeared. Only now and then one could be seen swinging from tree to tree, back into the deep forest, like great monkeys. Hawk-Eye again ran after his spear. This time he pulled it out of the wounded man's flesh himself, and left him rolling on the ground, too much hurt to attack him or defend himself. Then Hawk-Eye ran back to the little group hidden behind the rock.

Everything was now as quiet as if no one lived in the forest at all. There was not a single tree-dweller in sight except the first wounded man, and he was already crawling as fast as he could up the bluff.

In spite of everything, Hawk-Eye and Limberleg had held on to their meat, and now they felt the need of food. They cut Limberleg's load into four great chunks, and each took one. They ate as they walked. They ran along past the place where the mammoths were feeding and then turned their backs on the river and plunged into the deep forest toward the east. The ground began to rise a little, and Hawk-Eye said, "If we keep on climbing in the direction of the rising sun, we are bound to reach the blue hills at last."

All that day they journeyed, and that
night they spent in a tree. The next morning found them still climbing. At last, about
noon of the second day, they reached the
crest of the range and climbed out upon the
high, bald summit of the highest hill.

No one of their clan had ever been so far from the cave, and no one of them had ever seen what Hawk-Eye and Limberleg and the Twins now saw. There was the world spread out before them! They looked back far away in the blue distance toward the west, and there they saw a little silver thread. That silver thread was their river. They looked toward the south, and far, far away they saw more water than they had ever dreamed there was in the whole earth. They did n't know what it was. They were not even sure that it was water. They had never heard of the sea. They stood silent and breathless with wonder and gazed at it. At last Hawk-Eye said in an awestruck tone, "It's the end of the world."

"Let's go to the very edge and look over it," said Limberleg. "Maybe we can find out where the sun hides during the darkness."

You see what a brave woman she was.

"Then are these the blue hills?" asked Firetop. "They don't look blue a bit."

" The blueness is all around us, though,"
cried Firefly, pointing down into the valley.
"And beyond the end of the world, it's all
blue too, with sparkles on it! And the sky
is blue. The only place that is n't blue is
right around us."

"We will surely go through the blue

country to get to the end of the world then," said Firetop.

All this time Hawk-Eye had been standing on the highest point, studying the view and choosing landmarks. He knew how to find his way through forests as well as we know the way to the post-office. When he had the route all planned out, he called the children and Limberleg to his side. He pointed to the south. "Do you see far away that little neck of land which leads out to the very end of the world?" he said.. "We will keep the sun on this side of us the first half of the day and on the other side the other half of the day and we shall surely reach it. Then we shall see what lies beyond."

Hawk-Eye led the way over the crest of the hill and down into the forest below, the Twins and Limberleg close behind him. All day they pressed on, over hills, through dense woods, and across little streams, keeping always to the south. At last they found the narrow neck of land which they had seen from the hill-top. They camped that night in a tree, near the water's edge, and, at night-fall of the second day after, they climbed the last weary mile and stood upon the great rocks at the end of the world.

A stream of fresh water poured through a deep gorge beside them.

Toward the east and toward the west, farther than their eyes could see, stretched the dark blue waters. Toward the north they could look clear across the island to the distant shore of the mainland. We know now that they stood on the southern coast of the Isle of Wight, and that the faint blue line across the water would some day be called France. But the Twins and their father and mother thought that they stood on the very edge of the earth and looked out into mysterious regions which lay beyond.

As they stood gazing, the western sky flamed with red and gold and the sun sank out of sight behind a distant point of land. High up in the east the pale round disk of the moon hung in the deep blue of the sky. It was more wonderful than they had dreamed.

"To-morrow, if we wake early, we shall see where the sun comes from," said Limberleg.

They sat on the rocks and watched the stars come out and saw the moon sail away to the west, and then, when they were too weary to stay awake longer, they spread their skins on the rocks and slept under the open sky, with the boom of the surf for a lullaby.

VI
THE EARTHQUAKE

VI

THE EARTHQUAKE

I

THEY slept so soundly that they did not hear low rolling sounds of thunder or see the moon go out of sight behind a black cloud. Even lightning did not rouse them, but when at last the rain came splashing down over their bare skins they woke up. There was no shelter for them, so they huddled together in a wet heap and waited for the rain to be over and for the morning to come. It was no gentle spring shower.

The water poured down like a deluge. They were very wretched, and Firefly began to cry.

"Now, see here," Limberleg said to her, "there's water enough already! You need n't add your tears, or we shall all be drowned! The rain will be over some time. It won't hurt you."

When the lightning flashed, they could see the trees waving and bending in the wind and great breakers rolling up over the sandy beach.

But the rain was n't the worst that was to happen. After a while there came a strange shivering feeling in the rocks beneath them. It grew stronger and stronger till the whole earth shook and trembled.

Hawk-Eye and Limberleg had felt earthquakes before, but never one like this. It seemed as if the world were shaking itself to pieces. They huddled closer together and clasped their arms around the Twins.

"Oh," shrieked Limberleg, "the water gods are angry because we tried to find out the secret of the sun!" She and Hawk-Eye prayed to them at the top of their lungs. "Spare us, oh, spare us," they cried.

As they prayed, there came a long, fearful cracking noise, and the sound of falling rocks. It was as if the thunder had fallen to the earth and were rumbling round over it. A gigantic wave came roaring against the rocks as if it would dash them to pieces.

The Twins burrowed their heads in their mother's lap, and shook almost as if they were having little earthquakes of their own.

The great wave marked the crest of the storm. After that the winds grew gradually less violent, the rain ceased, and the waves crept farther and farther away down the beach.

The earth ceased its trembling. The clouds rolled away like great curtains, and the thunder went grumbling off toward the west.

When the gray dawn came stealing over the wet earth and the birds began to sing, Limberleg raised her head.

" Look," she said, "and listen ! The birds are singing! I thought the world had come to an end, but it is still here, and so are we."

Then they all opened their eyes, which they had kept shut for terror. A wonderful sight met them! Over the water toward the east the sky was blushing like a rose. Little pink clouds were hurrying away to lose themselves in the blue sky. Then the great fiery red disk of the sun rose slowly out of the water!

They watched it in awed silence as it climbed higher and higher into the blue. Then, trembling again with fear, the little group of watchers prostrated themselves before it in a blind impulse of worship.

When the sun was out of the water and up again in its regular place in the sky, all nature seemed so gay and joyous that the Twins and their father and mother forgot the fears of the night, and began to think about breakfast. They found it in the hollow of a rock far down the gorge.

The giant wave which had so frightened them, had left a fish flapping about in a little pool of water. When she saw it, Limberleg shouted: "The water gods are n't angry, after all! See, they have sent us a fine fish for our breakfast!"

Hawk-Eye quickly climbed down the steep rocks to the pool, caught the fish with his hands, killed it, and brought it back to Limberleg and the Twins.

While they were eating it, Limberleg seemed to be thinking hard. She was n't used to thinking, and she screwed up her face almost as if it hurt her. At last she said: "Listen to me! We now know what no one else in the world knows. We have found out what lies beyond the blue hills. We have gone to the end of the world and have looked over the edge, and have discovered the secret of the sun! We alone know that it hides beneath the waters during the darkness. There is no more for us to learn. Perhaps it would not be safe to know more, even if there were more to know! Let us go home."

"There is more to be learned about the hunting," said Hawk-Eye.

"We can find that out on our way back," said Limberleg.

"If there are going to be any more earthquakes, I'd rather be in the cave anyway," said Firefly. "Besides, I don't like the rain pouring over me. It's as bad as falling in the river."

Firetop said: "I'd like to get back to tell Squaretoes what I've seen. He's all the time telling about the wonderful things he can do. He's never seen the tree-people nor had an earthquake in his whole life. I guess I can make his eyes stick out."

Hawk-Eye said nothing, but he picked up the wet skins, shook them, bound them with thongs, and tied them to the shoulders of the others. Then each took his own weapons and they were ready to start.

II

From the point where they had spent the night, a chain of hills ran back inland. They followed these hills to the north for some miles and then, still keeping to the hill-tops, turned toward the west. In the late afternoon, under Hawk-Eye's skillful leadership, they came again to the place where they had crossed the isthmus that connected them with the mainland.

Hawk-Eye was some distance ahead of the others when he came out upon the high bluff that overlooked the channel and the isthmus. Suddenly he stopped with a cry of astonishment and stood still, his eyes staring.

Limberleg and the Twins rushed to his side.

"What is the matter?" they cried. For answer Hawk-Eye only pointed. Before them there was nothing but open water! A whole section of the neck of land which they had crossed only the day before had been swallowed up by the sea!

Where it had been, a mile of blue water now sparkled in the sun! They were completely shut off from the main land. When she realized what had happened, Limberleg sat heavily down on a log.

"The world isn't the same after all," she cried. "It's broken! Part of it has sunk beneath the waters!"

"Won't it ever get mended?" asked Firefly anxiously.

"Shan't we ever get back to the cave,
then?" cried Firetop.

"No," sobbed Limberleg. "We'll have
to stay here till we die."

Firefly whimpered a little and crept close
to her mother on the log, but Firetop noticed
that his father wasn't crying, so he swallowed several large lumps in his throat and

sat up straight. For some time they stayed on the bluff and looked down the steep banks of broken earth and rocks into the deep water below.

Great logs were floating about and huge trees, uprooted from the banks, were lying with their tops in the water.

At last Limberleg said in a discouraged voice, "Well, what shall we do?"

"The first thing to do," said Hawk-Eye, "is to go down to the beach and see what we can find to eat."

Beyond the steep cliffs on which they stood there was a bay with a wide beach. Beyond the bay great rocks extended in a chain out into the water. If you have been to England, you may have passed those very rocks. They are called "The Needles."

Hawk-Eye and Limberleg and the Twins climbed down to the beach. They were so hungry that they were almost ready to eat sand and pebbles, like chickens, if they could find nothing else.

But there was plenty of seaweed on the

beach and they found little mussels clinging
to it. They ate both the seaweed and the
mussels, as they walked along.

"See all the little holes in the sand,"
cried Firetop, when they were quite far
out on the beach. "Water spurts out of
them every time I step."

"Let's dig down and see what does it,"
said Firefly. "Maybe it's something good
to eat."

They took a large shell and scraped away the sand. They had never seen clams before, and Firefly got her finger pinched. Hawk-Eye opened a shell and ate one. He smacked his lips, and then he said, "Dig as many as you can, while I make a fire. Our supper is right here."

The Twins worked like beavers, while Hawk-Eye and Limberleg made a driftwood fire far back on the beach in a sheltered place near the cliffs.

Then Limberleg made a bed of seaweed in the coals and put in the clams as fast as the children brought them up from the sand. They must have steamed at least half a bushel! They ate every one, and I am quite sure this was the very first clam-bake that any one ever had in this world.

As they rested beside the fire after supper, warmed and fed, they began to feel more cheerful. Hawk-Eye said: "Anyway, we shall never be hungry while we stay here. Perhaps we shall like it just as well as we liked our forest cave."

Then Limberleg had a happy thought. "Do you know," she said, "I believe the water gods were lonesome and are glad that we came! They don't want us to go away again, and so they made the piece of land fall into the water to keep us here! You remember about that fish! I'm not afraid. I think they mean to take care of us."

And that was such a comforting thought that they went to sleep and slept soundly all night beside their drift-wood fire.

VII
THE ISLAND

VII

THE ISLAND

I

IF I were to tell you all the things that the Twins and their father and mother did on that island, it would make a book as big as the dictionary; so I can only tell you a very little about the wonderful days that followed. In the first place, they soon found out that it was a wonderful island. Small as it was, it had the most astonishing things in it.

There were great cliffs and jagged rocks along its coast in some places, and there were beautiful broad sandy beaches right next to them. The waves had washed holes clear through some of these great rocks and left them standing there like huge ruins.

The beaches were covered with star-fish

and beautiful shells and seaweed and crabs and jelly-fish and stones of all colors. The Twins found something new every time they played there.

Inland there were hills and valleys with sparkling streams of clear water running through them. There were sunny open meadows where bison grazed. In the woods there were deer and small game of all kinds, but though Hawk-Eye went everywhere in the days that followed the earthquake, he never saw a sign of a cave bear or of tigers or lions, or any of the more savage beasts which made life in their old home so full of terror.

Neither did he find a trace of any other human beings.

The season was early on the warm southern side of the island. The wild fruit trees were already in blossom, making the air sweet with fragrance, and giving promise of fruit later on.

There were all sorts of wild flowers and all kinds of trees in the woods, and every-

thing was so beautiful and seemed so safe
that it was easy to believe, as Limberleg
said, that the water gods did mean to take
care of them.

II

One day when Hawk-Eye and Limberleg had gone deer-hunting, Firetop and
Firefly climbed a high cliff on the east
coast to hunt for pigeons' eggs. From the
top of the hill, they could see for miles and

miles in every direction. The cliffs were on a long point of land, and behind the point was a deep bay, where all sorts of things could be picked up, when the tide was low. In a cleft of the rock Firetop found a nest with four eggs in it. He and Firefly were sitting on top of the hill eating them, when Firefly saw a queer black spot part way down the cliff, toward the east.

"What's that?" she said, pointing.

"Let's go and find out," said Firetop.

They climbed cautiously down to a lower level and worked their way through the bushes and vines which covered the sloping side of the bluff.

"It must be somewhere near here," said Firetop, "but I can't see it. It's hidden behind the bushes, whatever it is."

"Maybe it was a bear and he has moved," said Firefly, looking fearfully over her shoulder.

Of course they could not be quite sure there were no such creatures on the island.

"Pooh," said Firetop, "I'm not afraid. Come along."

They hunted up and down and sideways for some distance along the bluff, and were almost ready to give up, when a branch that Firetop was holding broke and he fell backward down the slope. He rolled over two or three times, and when he stopped rolling and sat up he was looking directly into the mouth of a great dark cave. A lot of stones and dirt came tumbling down with him, and, with that and some noise that Firetop made himself, there was quite a disturbance.

The cave was full of owls, and when the stones and dirt and a boy dropped in on them suddenly, they were very much surprised. No fewer than six of them flew out of the cave, and as they were blinded by the light, they bumped right into Firetop.

Those still in the cave flew about and beat their wings against the rocks. This made a terrible sound in the hollow cave, and besides that, they hooted. Firetop had never met an owl at such short range

before, and his red hair stood straight up
on his head, he was so scared. He beat
the owls off with his arms and yelled at the
top of his lungs.

Firefly heard him and came plunging
through the bushes after him. In another
minute she too had fallen through the same
place and landed beside Firetop. By the
time they had picked themselves up, the owls
had flown to a shelf on the rock, and there

they roosted in a row, staring solemnly at the Twins.

They neither moved nor spoke. Somehow the Twins expected them to speak and say something very reproving. They looked just that way. The Twins did n't wait to find out what it would be, however. They went crashing through the bushes and back to the top of the rock as fast as they could go.

That afternoon, when Hawk-Eye and Limberleg came home, bringing a young deer on their shoulders, the children told them about the cave and pointed it out from the top of the rock. Hawk-Eye at once threw down the deer and made a fire. Then he took a flaming torch in one hand and his spear in the other and started down the bluff.

"How did you get to the cave?" he asked Firetop.

"We went part way down the bluff and fell in," said Firetop.

Hawk-Eye laughed. "I'll see if I can't find a better way," he said.

He crept cautiously down the steep slope,
and when he reached the cave, he held his
torch above his head so as to light the inside of it, and with his other hand he held
his spear, ready to kill any wild animal that

might be living in it. It was just the sort of cave where one might expect to find wolves at least.

The owls came hooting out again just as they had when Firetop visited them, but nothing else stirred, and Hawk-Eye went boldly in. The cave was quite large, and as it was in a chalk cliff, it was white and clean except where the owls had made their nests.

Hawk-Eye did n't like the looks of owls. He did n't like their staring ways. So he tore up their nests and threw them down the bluff.

Then he came out of the cave and began to climb about on the slope, as if he were searching for something. It was not long before he gave a shout of joy and beckoned to Limberleg and the Twins, who were watching him eagerly.

They came bounding down the hillside at once. Hawk-Eye met them at the cave-entrance. "Here's our home," he said, pointing to the cave. "Nothing could be better. I have found a spring of fresh water near by! It is safer than any place we have ever found. Go in and see!"

Limberleg went in and looked all about. She was just as pleased with it as Hawk-Eye was. She did n't even say, "Let's see if we can't find another cave that suits us better."

She just threw her deer-skin down on the floor of the cave and laid her spear on one of the shelving rocks and began to live there right away. They always had their weapons with them, all of them. So there was nothing more to do but start a fire at the cave-mouth and begin to get supper. It was just as easy as moving into a furnished flat.

Hawk-Eye went back to the top of the hill and brought down the deer. He also brought some live fire-brands from the fire he had kindled. With these he started a new fire at the cave-mouth.

While Limberleg cut up the meat and the Twins broiled great pieces of it over the coals, Hawk-Eye took his stone axe and cut a rough path through the underbrush from the cave-entrance to the spring, and another to the hill-top. The paths were so hidden by tall weeds and bushes that they could run through them without being seen.

When at last they sat down beside the fire at the cave-entrance to eat their first dinner of roast venison in their new home, they felt as rich as—well it's really quite impossible to tell you just how rich they did feel.

VIII
THE RAFT

VIII

THE RAFT

When Limberleg woke the next morning, the bright sunshine was pouring into the cave, lighting up the very farthest corner of it. The vines which overhung the entrance were waving in the breeze, and their shadows were dancing gayly on the chalk floor.

Limberleg sat up and looked out. From the door she could see miles and miles of open water. To the north were the shores of England. Below was a beautiful sandy beach, and a little way from the shore there were rocks sticking out of the water. Gulls were wheeling and screaming about the rocks.

Limberleg took the gourd and went down the little green path to the spring for water. When she came back, the others were still sleeping. So she crept out through the path to the hill-top and gathered sticks to replenish the fire.

She was already broiling the venison when the others woke.

At breakfast, she said to Hawk-Eye, "I believe I will stay in the cave to-day, it is such a lot of work to start a new fire every day, and I can keep this one burning. Besides, the Twins must have new skins pretty soon. Those fox-furs they are now wearing are getting shabby. I will cure the deer-skin we brought home last night for them."

"We must get more skins," said Hawk-Eye. "We shall need them when cold weather comes. I will get the meat, and you can cook, and cure the skins, and tend the fire."

Then Hawk-Eye went off hunting, to be gone all day. The Twins ran down to the beach and went in wading. They were not so afraid of the water as they had been, but they stayed near shore because they could see great fish tumbling about in the waves, and they did n't know whether they ate children or not. Probably the fish did n't know, either. They had never had any to try. Anyway, the Twins thought they would not find out what their tastes were in the matter, and so they stayed near the shore, — or at least they meant to.

Ever since the great storm there had been logs and broken tree branches floating about in the water, and on this morning, the Twins found two of them bobbing about near the beach-line. They were not very large, and the Twins thought it would be fun to play with them. They waded out and pulled them in toward shore.

"Let's ride on these the way we rode that log in the river," said Firetop.

Firefly was always ready to do whatever Firetop did, so she got astride one, and Firetop mounted the other, and they went bouncing along through the water, half floating and half walking on the sandy bottom.

It was great fun, but the long branches stuck in the sand and scratched their legs, so they drew the logs nearer shore and

tried to pull off the branches. But some of them were too tough.

"We can twist them together," said Firetop. "That will keep them out of the way and maybe the logs won't roll so much."

They twisted the branches of the two logs roughly together, so they could not stick down into the water and then mounted their sea horses again and rode away. They were delighted to find that now the logs behaved much better, and they grew so bold that they ventured out into deeper water. They had made a wonderful plaything.

All the morning they rode the logs, and when the tide began to come in, they had the best time of all. It picked up the little raft and floated the children, screaming with joy, far up the beach on a long, low, rolling wave.

Limberleg had been so busy making a frame of sticks to stretch the deer-skin on that she had paid no attention to the Twins. But when she heard their screams, she came to the door of the cave and looked out on the beach. When she saw what they were doing, she came running down the bluff. She ran so fast she was all out of breath, but she gasped out: "You naughty, careless children! You must not do that any more — ever! You will certainly be eaten up by a big fish — or get drowned — or maybe both — if you do!" The Twins thought that their mother was very foolish, and, being cave twins, and not knowing any better, they said: "Aw, mother, we have been doing it all the morning, and never got drowned or eaten up once! Try it yourself and just see how easy it is."

But Limberleg was very unreasonable. She only said, "If you do it again, you know what will happen," and started back up the bluff. When she was out of sight, Firetop said: "Let's do it once more. She won't see us!" This shows just how wicked and disobedient cave children could be!

They pushed their raft out into the water and got on board. They were at the very farthest point from shore, when suddenly Limberleg came right out of the bushes and looked at them! When they saw her, the Twins were very much embarrassed. They thought perhaps they had better stay off shore a while.

They reached their feet down and dug their toes in the sand, but the tide was still coming in, and in spite of all they could do, it lifted them up and carried them right to where Limberleg stood. She looked at them very sternly. She had a switch in her hand. She said: "I told you what would happen! I shall have to punish you, but it hurts me worse than it hurts you." I sup-

pose that was the first time any parent ever
said that. Then she began to use the switch
on their bare legs.

Perhaps you never have been switched
on your wet bare legs, so I 'll explain that
it hurts. Firetop and Firefly did n't under-
stand how it could hurt her more than it
did them. However, they did n't say so.
They just ran for the cave as fast as they
could go. But I have already told you that
Limberleg could run faster than anybody
and she kept right up with them all the way.

When they were in the cave again, any

one passing by would certainly have thought from the sounds that a pack of wildcats lived there. At last Limberleg said to them, "Now, you see, I will be minded," and then she made them sit still in the corner of the cave until she had finished the wooden frame and stretched the deer-skin over it.

I suppose that if she had been a reasonable and kind mother she would have let them go on and get drowned or eaten up by a shark. But she was n't, and so they were n't, or else you can very well see that this story would have had to end right here.

When Hawk-Eye came home that afternoon with two live rabbits which he had snared, the Twins were so delighted with them that they forgot all about their troubles of the morning.

"Can't we keep the rabbits alive?" they begged.

"How can you keep them?" said Hawk-Eye. "They 'll run away."

"We can tie them by their legs," said Firetop.

"We can cut sticks and drive them down in the ground, and keep the rabbits inside the sticks," cried Firefly.

"What will you cut them with?" asked Hawk-Eye.

"With your stone axe," Firefly answered as quick as a wink.

Hawk-Eye looked very solemn. "Will you be sure to bring it back to the cave, if I let you take my axe?" he said.

"Of course," cried the Twins. They took the axe at once and rushed out to begin the fence of sticks, while Hawk-Eye tied the rabbits by their hind legs to a little tree near the cave.

When they finished the fence the next day, I regret to say the stone axe was nowhere to be found, and it was three days before it turned up under a bush where they had cut sticks.

While the children were busy fencing in the rabbits, Limberleg told Hawk-Eye about the raft.

"You can see it down there on the beach," she said. "I really think it was very clever of them to make such a thing, but of course I didn't tell them so."

"*Of* course not," said Hawk-Eye.

Now, wasn't that just like parents?

Pretty soon, while Limberleg was cooking supper, Hawk-Eye slipped down to the beach by himself and took a look at the raft. Then he dragged it down to the water and tried it himself. He tried it several times. He didn't say anything about it when he got back to the cave, but the Twins saw how very clean his skin looked. And they nodded knowingly at each other. They had their suspicions.

IX
THE SURPRISE

IX

THE SURPRISE

WHAT with fish and clams and crabs and periwinkles and roots and game and berries and wild plums and all sorts of other good things to eat, as the summer came on, the Twins and their father and mother began to grow fat.

Limberleg did n't go hunting as she used to. There was no need of it now, for Hawk-Eye could bring home more game than they needed. So she stayed by the cave and kept the hearth fire bright and cooked the food and cured the skins and looked after the children.

The Twins kept the rabbits and fed them every day with fresh leaves and roots, and by and by there were six baby rabbits in the cage too.

"We might make the cage larger and

have more rabbits," said Hawk-Eye, "and then in winter, we should always have plenty of fresh meat right at hand."

"What a good idea!" said Limberleg. "The children can feed them."

"Yes," said Hawk-Eye, "if they don't forget it."

"I'll see that they don't forget it," said Limberleg.

The Twins heard her say it.

"I think probably she will," said Firetop. He had great confidence in his mother.

"Will what?" said Firefly.

"Will see that we don't forget it," said Firetop, and they guessed right. She did.

By July they had a large enclosure fenced off and ever so many rabbits in it. For cave people they were now very rich. They had a fine cave home, plenty of skins, and plenty of food.

Limberleg had made herself a good needle out of bone and had sewed nice soft deer-skins into clothes for them, all ready for cold weather. She had even made beautiful necklaces of shells for Firefly and herself.

One summer evening, as they sat looking at the moon, Limberleg said: "You see I was right about the water gods. There have n't been any more earthquakes, and we have everything we want to eat, and plenty of warm skins and a fine cave to live in. There is just one thing more I want. I don't care much for society, but I should like more people to talk to."

"I wish Grannie and the rest were here," said Firetop. "I should like to show Square-toes our rabbits."

"And I should like to show Robin my necklace," said Firefly.

"It's no use wishing," said Firetop. "There's all that water."

Hawk-Eye, as usual, said nothing, but all the time he was thinking hard about the floating log that the Twins had crossed the river on, and the raft they had made of the two floating trees.

It was not long after this that Limberleg began to notice that though he was gone all day every day, Hawk-Eye often came home without game. One day she heard the sound of his stone axe, as if he were cutting down a tree, but she thought nothing more about it.

After that she heard the sound of the axe every day for many days. It seemed to come from the bay behind the point of land. At last she said to him: "What in the world are you doing with your axe? I hear such a pounding every day." Hawk-Eye did not tell her what he was making. He only said, "Maybe some day, when I get it done, you will see."

The Twins heard the axe too, and they made up their minds they were going to find out what was going on. The next day, as they were playing in their cave back of their bluff at low tide, Firefly saw a little column of smoke rising out of the woods near the place where a small stream flowed into the bay. She also heard the axe. The sound seemed to come from somewhere near the

smoke. She pointed the smoke out to Firetop, and the two children ran swiftly around
the beach and up the little stream for a short
distance.

There they found Hawk-Eye. He was
working away at the log of a good-sized
tree which he had cut down. He had made
the log almost flat on one side by chipping
off pieces with his axe, and he had shaped
the ends a little. Now he was hollowing out
the inside. He was doing this partly with
his axe and partly by burning it.

Hawk-Eye was working so busily he did
not know that any one was near him until
Firetop called out, "What are you making,
Father?"

Hawk-Eye stopped chopping. "It's a
secret," he said. "If I tell you, you'll tell."

"No, we won't. Anyway, there's no one
to tell but Mother," said Firefly.

"She's just the one I want to keep it
from," said Hawk-Eye. "It's a surprise."

"Oh, well, if it is a surprise, of course we
won't tell," said Firetop.

" Do you know what it is, or is it a surprise to you too?" asked Firefly.

" Maybe it is," said Hawk-Eye. " I 'm not sure yet. When I get the inside of this log all cut out, I 'm going to see if it will float without rolling over. Maybe I can get in it and make it go where I want it to. If I can, then all sorts of things may happen, but you must *not* tell Mother."

" Why?" asked Firefly. " Would n't she let you play with it?"

" Maybe not," said Hawk-Eye.

" You 'd better be careful," said Firefly, shaking her head, " or you know what will happen!"

Hawk-Eye laughed and went on chopping. Every day after that the Twins followed their father to the little cove and watched him work. Every evening they nearly burst trying not to tell. One day when they went down to the cove, they found their father taking out the last chips from the inside of the log.

"When the tide comes in, it backs up into

the stream," said Hawk-Eye, "and the next
time it does it, I'm going to push the log
into the water and then out into the bay. If
it floats right side up, I am going for a ride."

"How will you push it?" asked Firetop.
"Are you going to let your legs hang over
and hitch yourself along that way?"

"I shan't need any turtles to bite me
to make me go anyway," said Hawk-Eye.
"I'm going to push it with a pole."

The pole was already in the log. The tide began to flow in. As soon as the water was deep enough Hawk-Eye pushed the log into the water. It floated, of course. Hawk-Eye waded along beside it into deeper water. Then he undertook to get aboard, but he put his weight too much on one side. It rolled over, and he rolled with it, and went splash on his stomach right into the water! Firetop and Firefly danced on the beach with glee.

Hawk-Eye got up all dripping wet and tried again. This time he stepped into the middle of the boat. He got safely in, but it was still very tippy, so he put sand in the bottom of it and made it heavier. Then he tried again.

It was a proud moment when at last he took his pole and pushed off.

"I'm going to keep close to shore and go around the point if I can," he said.

The children tore up the bank and over the hill to get back to the cave in time to see him coming. Limberleg was weaving

a berry basket out of strips of bark, when the children came racing into the cave. They were so excited they could n't keep still.

"What in the world is the matter with you?" cried Limberleg, at last. "You've been running to the edge of the bluff and back again ever since you came in. What are you looking at?"

"At that! at that!" shrieked Firetop, pointing down to the water.

There, coming close to the shore around the bend, was Hawk-Eye in the very first boat that was ever made — in that part of the world at least.

Limberleg was so astonished that she could n't speak. She dashed down the side of the bluff without stopping for the path, and the Twins came tumbling after her. Of, course, Limberleg got there first. She always did. And when the Twins reached the water's edge, she was already in the boat with Hawk-Eye. She was certainly a brave woman!

X
THE VOYAGE

X
THE VOYAGE

AFTER Limberleg had had a ride, the Twins took a turn, while their mother watched them from the shore.

"It's almost more fun than our logs," said Firetop, when he took his first ride.

They played with the boat and tried all sorts of experiments with it, and were so happy and excited that it grew dark and the moon came out before one of them so much as thought of anything to eat.

For days and days after that, Hawk-Eye worked on his boat. He found out all its tricks. He even found out that he could go in deep water if he paddled. He found it out first by using his hands for oars. Then he chopped out a clumsy flat paddle.

All this took him some time, but by mid-summer he had become quite expert with his clumsy craft. He could keep it right side up and make it go where he wanted it to at any rate.

Sometimes he ventured out into the deep water around the gulls' rocks. One day he even rowed all round them. He could look down into the water and see shoals of fish swimming about, but he could not catch them.

When he went back to the cave that day, he said to Limberleg: "I have an idea. Why can't you weave a kind of net out of leather thongs? I can fasten it in the water out by the rocks and catch fish in it. The water gods may like us very much, as you say, but they haven't been throwing any fish up on land for us since the earthquake, so I'm going to try to catch some."

"To be sure," said Limberleg. "We snare rabbits, why shouldn't we snare fish?"

They had made hooks out of bone and had caught river fish sometimes when they lived back in the forest, but they had not brought any hooks with them on their journey. They had always been more used to hunting game than to fishing, anyway. Now with a sea full of fish right at hand, waiting to be caught, they began to think more about it.

"If we could catch fish, we should have more food right at hand than we could possibly eat, without ever hunting at all, if we didn't want to," said Hawk-Eye.

After that Limberleg spent days and days tying leather thongs together in a coarse net, while Hawk-Eye made bone fish-hooks for himself and Limberleg and the Twins, and fastened them to long fine strings of leather.

By August, Hawk-Eye had taught the Twins how to fish the streams for trout, and he himself had learned how to fasten his net between two of the gull rocks and catch the fish that swam in deep water.

There was nothing Hawk-Eye liked so much as going out in his boat. He went up and down the coast for miles, and it was not long before he knew every little creek and inlet and bay on the eastern end of the island.

At last, one day in August, he said to Limberleg: "I am going to load the boat with food to last a few days and see if I can't get over to the mainland. It is only a short distance across to the nearest point. I've been farther than that in my boat already."

"But I am afraid you'll be drowned," cried Limberleg, "and then what shall we do?"

"You can take care of yourselves," said Hawk-Eye. "The children can already fish in the streams, and there are the rabbits and the clams. You will not want for anything while I am away."

"But we shall be lonesome," cried Limberleg; "and suppose you should never come back!"

"But I shall come back," said Hawk-Eye. "You'll see."

Limberleg knew it was useless to say any more, and the very next day she and the Twins helped him load his boat with deer-meat and wild plums and acorns, and then Hawk-Eye put in his spear and his stone axe and hooks and line, and got in himself.

The three of them stood on the beach and watched him push off from their island and start across the channel toward the main land. They watched him until the boat was a mere black speck in the distance. Then they trudged slowly back to their lonely cave.

There followed many anxious days and nights. Limberleg went back to hunting again. She took the Twins with her, and began to teach them to hunt like men.

"If anything should happen to me, you could take care of yourselves if you knew how to hunt and trap as well as fish," she said.

Beside getting food for their daily needs, they began to store it for the winter. They gathered nuts by the bushel and piled them in heaps in the corner of the cave. Whenever they were not sleeping or doing anything else, they were always gathering wood for the fire.

In this way four long weeks went by. At
last came a day when the wind was sharp,
and it seemed as if summer were nearly
over.

Limberleg and the Twins had gone down
to the cave behind their bluff to get clams
for supper. They had one of Limberleg's
baskets with them, and had nearly filled it
with clams. They were out some distance
from the beach-line, for the tide was low.

Suddenly the water began to rise. The
returning tide came in such a flood that
they had to run as fast as their legs could
carry them to get safely ashore. They had

reached the bank and were just beginning to climb slowly up the bluff, when they heard a shout behind them. Limberleg was so startled that her knees gave way under her and she sat right down in the basket of clams!

They looked across the cove, and there, coming in with the tide, was their own boat, with brave Hawk-Eye in it waving his hand to them. They could see three other heads beside Hawk-Eye's, but neither Limberleg nor the Twins could tell whose heads they were. They left the basket of clams on the side of the bluff and tore down to the water's edge.

As the boat came near the shore, they saw Grannie, looking scared to death, sitting in the bottom of the boat, and holding on to each side with all her might. Behind her were Blackbird and Squaretoes!

The moment the boat came near shore, the two boys tumbled out of the back end of it, nearly upsetting Grannie, and splashed through the shallow water to the shore.

They butted Firetop in the stomach and
knocked him flat, and spun Firefly around
in the sand to show how glad they were to
see them.

When at last the prow of the boat grated
on the sand, and Grannie and Hawk-Eye
got out, the four children ran round them
in circles like puppies, screaming with joy.
Even Limberleg danced. Grannie clapped
her hands over her ears.

When the noise had calmed down a little, she seized Firetop and Firefly and shook them soundly.

"You little red-headed wretches," she cried. "Here you are alive and well, and fat as rabbits, and all this time I've worried the heart nearly out of me wondering what had become of you!"

It had been such a long time since the spring morning when the Twins had stolen away out of the cave that at first they did not know what Grannie was talking about. They had never thought how she must have felt when she found that they were gone.

Hawk-Eye laughed. "I've brought Grannie back with me on purpose to give you what you deserve," he said. "She told me she was going to take a stick to you as soon as she saw you, for playing such a trick on her."

"Just you wait until I get a stick," cried Grannie. She looked fierce as she said it, but the Twins knew very well she was just

as glad to see them as they were to see
her. They seized her hands, one on each
side, and began to pull her up the hill.
Blackbird and Squaretoes pushed from
behind.

"Go along with you," screamed Grannie, holding back with all her might. "I
can't run so fast; I am all out of breath."

"We 'll run you, then," screamed the children, and they pulled and pushed until they got her panting and breathless to the top of the hill. Hawk-Eye had drawn his precious boat high up on the beach out of reach of the tide, and he and Limberleg followed more slowly with the basket of clams.

At the top of the hill, the Twins, with Blackbird and Squaretoes, ducked into the hidden path that led to the cave, just like mice diving down a mouse-hole.

Grannie was left standing alone on the hill-top. She could n't see what had become of the children. She could hear their voices, and down the bluff she could see a thin column of smoke rising. She knew the cave must be there, but she did n't know how to get to it.

When Hawk-Eye and Limberleg came up, they took her with them through the little green alley that led to the cave. When they reached it the children had flung a great pile of dry sticks on the fire, and the flames

were leaping high in the air to welcome
them.

"See," cried Limberleg, "even the fire
dances with joy at your coming."

She took Grannie into the cave and
showed her the piles of warm skins, and
the heaps of nuts: then she showed Grannie how to cook clams.

The Twins had taken Blackbird and Squaretoes the very first thing to see the rabbits. Then they came back for Grannie and made her go and see them too, and when every one had seen everything there was to see, it was dark, and Limberleg had a real feast ready for them to eat.

She had killed a deer the day before, and so they had broiled venison, seasoned with sea salt. They had clams steamed with sea-weed, and they had nuts and wild plums.

When they had all stuffed themselves full, Limberleg said to Hawk-Eye: "Now tell us all about your journey. When you went away, we watched you from the hill-top until you were a mere speck on the water. We knew nothing more of you until we heard your shout to-day. There were many weary days between."

"They were not weary to me," said Hawk-Eye. "I reached the other shore in safety, and then turned my boat toward the sunset. I kept in the shallow water near the shore, and followed the coast around the end of the point of land which we crossed when we came here.

"I knew our river must empty into the big water not far away, and so I paddled up the first stream I found. I slept in the boat at night. The first night I was awakened by the howling of wolves. But I had only to push my boat out into the stream. They would not follow me there.

"For two days I paddled up-stream. The second day I began to see things that I knew, and on the morning of the third I reached the river path just as Grannie was coming down for water."

"Yes, yes," cried Grannie. "I thought I was dreaming! The boat frightened me. I thought Hawk-Eye was dead and that I saw his spirit. I started to run to the cave."

"Did you think we were all dead?" asked Limberleg.

"Yes," said Grannie. "I thought some cave bear or tiger had got you. You were always so bold and venturesome. And as for these worthless ones," she added, patting Firetop on the head, "I did n't know whether they had gone with you, or had stolen away into the woods and been eaten by old Saber-tooth."

"Well, you see," cried Limberleg, laughing, "it pays to be bold and brave." When she said "bold and brave," she looked right at Hawk-Eye. She thought he was the boldest and bravest man in the world.

"There are n't any saber-toothed tigers on this island, and there's plenty to eat every day. Did n't the others want to come too when you told them about it?" she said to Hawk-Eye.

"They all wanted to come," Hawk-Eye answered, "but the boat would not hold so many. So I stayed to show them how to make boats for themselves. Long Arm and Big Ear and Gray Wolf are all at work on them now, and they will come in the spring or summer if they get them done."

"How will they know the way?" asked Firetop.

"I told them just how to follow the river

161

and the coast, and where to cross," said Hawk-Eye. "They can't help finding the island, and if they find the island, they can't help finding us. I told them we were on the side where the sun rises out of the water."

It had grown very dark as they talked. There was only firelight in the cave, but just then Limberleg saw a bright streak on the edge of the water toward the east.

"Look, Grannie, look," she cried, pointing to it. "We have discovered the secret of the sun and the moon! They both sleep in the water!"

The children and Grannie and Hawk-Eye and Limberleg all watched together until the white streak grew brighter and stretched in a silver path across the water to the beach below. They saw the pale disk of the moon slowly rise into the deep blue of the night sky, and the stars wink down at them.

"I suppose no one else in the whole world knows the secret," said Limberleg solemnly. "You see this is the end of the world. You can't go any farther."

"Except in my boat," said Hawk-Eye.

"The spirits of the water have been good to us," said Limberleg. "We will not tempt them too far. If there are more secrets, we will not try to find them out."

"Some day," said Hawk-Eye, "some day I mean to go "— but Limberleg would not let him finish.

"NO," she said, putting her hand over his mouth, "no, you are not going anywhere at all, ever again! You are going to stay right here with us and be happy."

L'ENVOI

Long, long ago, when the Earth was young
And Time was not yet old,
Ere all the stars in the sky were hung,
Or the silver moon grown cold;

When the clouds that sail between the worlds
Were fanned with fluttering wings,
And over all the land there curled
The fronds of growing things:

When fishes swarmed in all the seas,
And on the wooded shore
There roamed among the forest trees
A million beasts or more;

Then in the early morn of Time,
Called from the formless clod,
Came Man, to start the weary climb
From wild beast up to God,--

Oh, bravely did he dare and do,
And bravely fight and die,
Or you to-day could not be you,
And I could not be I.